ISLAND HERITAGE™
PUBLISHING
A DIVISION OF THE MADDEN CORPORATION

94-411 Kōʻaki Street
Waipahu, Hawaiʻi 96797-2806
Orders: (800) 468-2800
Information: (808) 564-8800
Fax: (808) 564-8877
welcometotheislands.com

ISBN: 1-61710-170-2
First Edition, Twelfth Printing—2017
COP 171007

A COCONUT NAMED BOB

written by Austin Weaver

illustrated by Don Robinson

ISLAND HERITAGE™
PUBLISHING

On a sun-drenched island lived a lonely little boy. He had few friends besides his dad and the fishermen on the wharf.

Most of the time, he worked for the fishermen, selling their catch in the market. When there were no fish to sell, he gathered coconuts the way his father had taught him.

He walked along the beach until he found the right tree, then he climbed its rough trunk. Sitting among the branches, he picked coconuts one by one and threw them down to the sand below.

One day as the boy was working in a tree, a certain coconut caught his eye. He twisted it loose, turned it around and around, looking closely at it. Somehow he knew there was something special about this coconut. He put it aside and continued his work.

When the boy was
finished, he slid down the
tree and loaded all the coconuts
into a burlap bag. He headed to the
market and sold every coconut -- but one.

He ran home tired but eager. Under the setting sun, he took the coconut behind his house and set it on a log. He disappeared into a weathered old shed and came out holding two cans of paint. The boy pried the lid off of a can of red paint, dipped his brush into it, and gave the coconut a mouth. Next, he grabbed a can of green paint and painted two round eyes.

He looked closely at the coconut's
new face and smiling he
whispered, "Your name is Bob."

The boy took Bob wherever he went. When they went to the movies, Bob sat in the cup holder. When they went to the beach, Bob sat on the boy's towel and watched the boy splash in the waves. And when the boy went sailing with his father, Bob went too. Sometimes he would roll around on the deck and sometimes he would just sit on top of the folded sail.

One day while the boy and his father were sailing to a nearby island, Bob sat basking in the sun. The day was warm, the boat rocked gently back and forth, and ever so slowly, Bob fell fast asleep.

The sky grew dark with clouds, but Bob's eyes were closed and he didn't see them. The wind grew loud and frightening, but Bob didn't hear it because the boy had not painted him any ears. The boat was tossed wildly back and forth, but Bob didn't wake up. Suddenly a wave crashed over the side and washed Bob overboard. The boy screamed and ran to the side of the boat! Fearing that the boy would jump in after his friend, his father caught him and held him tight. The boy cried and cried while his father held him close.

The angry sea tossed Bob into the troughs and over the crests of the waves and carried him farther and farther away from his boy. It was a long night, and Bob was terrified. After a while, the rain stopped and the wind died down. A drop of water rolled down Bob's face. It wasn't the cold seawater; it was a tear. The boy was gone, and Bob was alone.

Next morning the boy got up, dried tears on his face. He sat on the edge of the boat and began to cry again, letting his tears fall into the water. The sky was grey and the wind was cold, but the storm was over. That night, the boy sat on deck gazing up at the stars. He thought about Bob, but there were no more tears.

Bob floated on the sea for many days. One afternoon when the sun was high, an island the size of a pea appeared on the horizon. By the time the sun was setting, it was the size of a pancake. By the next morning, Bob was resting on the island's beautiful sandy beach. He didn't know how to feel. His boy was lost, he was alone on a strange island, and something green was growing out of him. Bob didn't know it, but he was becoming a tree.

Every day he grew taller and taller. When the wind blew, Bob's thin trunk bent and swayed.

When it stormed, Bob's small palm branches drooped in the rain.

Days turned into weeks,
weeks into months, and
months into years.

Bob became a proud figure of
a tree. Now when the wind
blew, Bob's sturdy trunk
stood strong and straight,
and when it rained, it was
nothing but a refreshing
drink. He thought about his
boy often, but he didn't cry
any more.

For a while, Bob's life was quiet and lonely. He was the only palm tree on the island. Then late one afternoon, just as the sun was disappearing beyond the horizon, Bob caught a glimpse of something being tossed in the surf not far down the beach. He couldn't see what it was in the fading sunlight.

Next morning, as the sun rose over the ocean, Bob looked down the beach again. If he had been a boy instead of a palm tree, he would have jumped for joy. A coconut was resting in the sand.

Years flew by like the wind. Bob was a happy tree. More coconuts floated to the island and grew into neighboring trees. He looked forward to seeing them every morning. During the day, Bob loved to watch dolphins play in the shallows and little crabs scurry across the sand. Bob's life was a good one, but even after all the years, he still wished his boy could be a part of it.

One bright sunshiny day Bob was watching the crabs and dolphins when he happened to glance out over the ocean. He saw seagulls diving for fish, and farther away, something else. Almost not believing his eyes, Bob blinked and looked again. There on the horizon was a sailboat the size of a pea. By evening, it was the size of a pancake, and in the morning Bob saw a beautiful little boat anchored right off his sandy beach.

The boat had not been there long before an old man and his family started for the beach. When they reached the island, the old man's grandchildren chased each other across the sand while the adults set out a picnic lunch.

One of the boys ran over to Bob and looked up at his branches full of coconuts. He climbed Bob's trunk and began picking coconuts. The boy had only been in the tree a short time when a certain coconut caught his eye. He twisted it loose, turned it around and around, looking closely at it. He put it aside and continued his work.

When he finished, he climbed down the tree, picked up the coconut and ran to his grandfather. "Look, Granddad, there's something special about this coconut!" The old man took the coconut from his grandson and looked at it closely, as if remembering something. He retraced the boy's footsteps with his eyes and saw the tree his grandson had climbed. With tears in his eyes, the old man walked slowly toward the tree as if walking back in time.

For a while he stood quietly looking up into its branches, thinking of years gone by. Then a smile spread across his face, and he gently reached out and touched the tree.

Smiling he whispered, "Hello, Bob. How have you been?"

The End